I0537714

Cantona - Ooh Ah

Geoffrey Howard

Cantona - Ooh Ah

Geoffrey Howard

Pendlebury Press Limited

pendleburypress@virginmedia.com

Amazon: Sole Distributor and Printer

ISBN: 978-0-9935945-5-7

DEDICATION

I dedicate the first of these two short pieces to Eric Cantona and the second to two of my grandchildren Keira and Jack who are happiest with a ball at their feet.

CONTENTS

Foreword   i

1   Cantona – Ooh Ah   1

2   Own Goal   22

Foreword

The first piece, *Cantona - Ooh Ah* is written as a tribute to one of football's all-time greats. It is in recognition of the fact that in the view of fans, there is something mysterious and other-worldly about Mr. Cantona. I have tried to reflect this in a rather tongue in cheek way.

The references to Eric Cantona, a Pope, Vatican officials, a bishop and a second cousin of Eric Cantona are fictional and do not have any bearing on reality. I hope the living will receive what I have written in the spirit in which it was intended. I have chosen common names for other characters in the story. These are fictional and are not based on anyone alive or dead.

The second piece, *Own Goal,* is a short sketch written for film. It may not be performed without consent. Please contact pendleburypress@virginmedia.com for terms.

Cantona –Ooh Ah

One Day in May 2017

Pope Francis was at the breakfast table, eating a boiled egg and toast. A large espresso was half drunk. The butler tapped on the door and came in. "Your Holiness, Cardinal Abrego is here."

"Bring him in, Enrico, and get him coffee." The butler ushered in the cardinal and left the room. "Javier, so early. Take a seat," said his Holiness in Spanish. The cardinal sat opposite the Pope at the breakfast table, pulled a bag of jelly beans from his pocket and reached across the table offering one to His Holiness.

"Jorge, your favourite," he said in a Buenos Aires accent.

"Jelly footballers! Which one is Lionel Messi?"

"None of him left."

"You always eat the best ones!"

"The blue ones are very nice. Mascherano." The Pope took one and put it on the table.

"I'll have it after my breakfast."

"Jorge," said the cardinal, "You know there can be only one God?"

"Javier, do you mean God or *God*?" he asked, eating a spoonful of egg. The butler walked in and put the coffee in front of the cardinal and left.

"I mean *God.*"

"Ah! So you mean there can only be one *God*. Javier, you're in charge of the Congregation for the Doctrine of the Faith. Why do you state the obvious? At first, I thought you meant there can only be one God."

"No. I mean *God.* The cardinal took an orange jelly footballer from the bag and popped it into his mouth. "Arjan Robben." While chewing on it, he said, "Well, the God who isn't really *God* has re-emerged."

"You mean God?"

"Yes, God."

"Javier, that's for you to deal with. It's too risky for me to get involved."

"Too risky for you, Jorge! What about me?"

"I'm the only one who can fire you. Draft something."

"It might backfire. *We* could be seen as the heretics."

*　　*　　*

July 7th 1968

"Alex, Shay, Bill, David, Bob, Pat, Bobby, Nobby, George, Brian, John, I baptize you ..." Father Ó Bradáin scooped water from the font and poured it on the head of the baby. "In the name of the Father and of the son." He paused again and scooped water onto the head of the child. "And of the Holy Spirit." Father Ó Bradáin looked at Brogan Quirke. "I bet he was born on

29th of May."

Brogan beamed. "I can see you are a believer. Keep saying your prayers for them, Father." Father Ó Bradáin handed the child back to Aoife Quirke. From there, she pushed the pram with Brogan the short distance to Old Trafford football ground. Brogan proudly held the child in the scarlet Christening robe in front of the ground, while his brother Niall took photographs. Brogan was a happy man. Not only had his wife given him a son on 29th May, but Manchester United won the European cup that day, beating Benfica 4-1. Brogan took the child to his first match, before he was six years old.

*   *   *

March 9th 2017

The restaurant, *La Marseillaise*, on Ayres Road, was empty but for a man and woman in their 70s, dressed as if for a special occasion. The chef had been Christened Bobby, along with his other ten names, but was known as Bob to friends and Robert by his clientele, pronounced in the French way - *Row-Bair!* It sounded better that way.

"Waiter, this duck is quacking," said the man, "and the cow is mooing. I wanted well done."

"The filet and duck *are* well done, Sir," replied Jean-Luc, the proprietor, "but I will ask chef to cook them longer."

"And can I have the salt and pepper, please?"

said the man. Jean-Luc Cantona took the plates of food into the kitchen. The couple chatted for a moment, but then *Row-Bair* burst in from the kitchen and went to the till. He printed out the bill, ripped it from the printer and strode up to the couple.

"One bottle of Bollinger," he said angrily in his Manchester accent. "Scallops, soup, filet de boeuf, duck breast, one St Emilion Grand Cru Classé, 1990. Four hundred and twenty three pounds and ninety four pence!" he shouted, holding up the till receipt in front of the man's face. He tore it in half and threw it on the table. "I don't want your money! And don't insult me by asking for salt and pepper! My food is perfectly seasoned. And I cook! If you want cremation go to an undertaker! You look ready for it. Get out!"

Jean-Luc ouzed embarrassment as he retrieved their coats, and hurriedly helped them to put them on. The couple scuttled onto the street without a word. Bob locked the door behind them and turned the sign to "Closed." A half of the Bollinger remained in the ice bucket next to the table. The bottle of St Emilion had not been touched. Bob brought two clean champagne flutes and put them on the laid table. The men sat down there and poured the champagne which they drank as they talked.

"I'm going back to Marseille," said Jean-Luc.

"To do what?"

"Paint."

"No one wants copies of old masters!" said Bob.

Jean-Luc, was from Marseille and a year older than Bob. He had studied Renaissance painting at the School of Fine Art, Paris. His work was in the style of the old masters and he loathed all art after the 17th century. To this day, he has hundreds of canvasses in store on an industrial estate - Zone D'Activités Arnavant, outside Marseille.

"I've got to do something," said Jean-Luc. Twenty covers a week doesn't pay the bills. We're out of cash."

"Then let's sell up and both go back to Marseille, but not for you to die of hunger in an attic. We can get restaurant work."

"It's a pity it has to end up like this, but you are right."

"Let's stay on till after 24th June. I want to go to a charity match. Your second cousin is coming back to Manchester."

"Eric?"

Bob went to the bar and brought back a copy of the Manchester Evening News. He read, "The Manchester United Legend is returning to play in a celebrity football match. Other players will include celebrities from sport and entertainment. Mr. Cantona's stay in Manchester will span three days, during which he will raise money for local and national charities."

"O.K, let's see if the bank will let us take some equity out of this place while we're waiting to sell."

"You hungry?" asked Bob.

"Famished." Bob went into the kitchen to

fetch the two plates, while Jean-Luc poured the St Emilion. Bob returned holding two plates.

"Duck or filet?"

"Filet." Bob put the filet in front of Jean-Luc and sat opposite.

"Bob, I need to get this place up for sale and raise some cash. I'm gonna be busy for a couple of weeks. You've not had a break for years. Why don't you go somewhere warm while I sort things out. We'll close for a couple of weeks."

*   *   *

Bob's love of food came from his love of football. The smell of fried onions from hot dog sellers on match day was inseparable from the beautiful game. In childhood, when United weren't playing, his nose sniffed the air with disappointment. Approaching the age of ten, he asked for a bag of onions for his birthday. From then on, most days smelled like match days. His mother gave him free rein of the kitchen. Onions with fried potatoes, onions with tinned spaghetti, onions on toast – fried onions with anything.

Out of work at the age of 19, Bob borrowed £100 from his father to go fruit picking in France. When the fruit season ended, he got a job at the Café Légionaire Bleu, Marseille, where he became the cleaner – toilets, cookers, floors, windows, paintwork and pavements. It took fifteen years to work his way up to chef, acquiring a Michelin star after a further nine years.

Hi business partner, Jean-Luc, tried to earn a living as an artist after leaving art school, but failed. At the age of 35, weary of living off his mother, and various girlfriends, he, too, became cleaner at the Café Légionaire Bleu – toilets, cookers, floors, windows, paintwork and pavements. After a year, and evening classes, he became a waiter. In his spare time, he churned out even more canvasses that no one would buy - copies Caravaggio, Botticelli and Guido Reni.

For years, he and Robert had a cigarette together just before opening time. They chatted about women, football and Jean-Luc's controlling mother, a woman in her 80s, who smoked cheap cigarettes and was a member of the Front National.

Early one evening in late autumn, Jean-Luc and Bob walked out of the restaurant an hour before opening time and sat at a table on the restaurant terrace. Bob held out a packet of Gauloise. Jean-Luc took one. Bob held out his lighter. Both men lit up, inhaled and blew out smoke. A young woman walked past. Their heads moved as one from right to left.

"I am opening a restaurant. I will give you 49% of the ownership if you will join me as chef."

"You're broke."

"Maman is dead."

"Dead? You should be at home."

"To do what? Grieve? The woman who has tried to manipulate me all my life is dead and you tell me to grieve! She wrecked every relationship I ever had! I'm not mourning."

Jean-Luc gained a modest amount from the sale of his mother's apartment, shared with his brother, but not enough to set up a restaurant in the style that Bob wanted, but the idea had appeal. Something was missing from Bob's world and he wanted to get it back – the smell of fried onions, but not in his kitchen.

The Marseillaise opened a few months later. Bob had wanted a Manchester city centre location or upmarket Didsbury, but they couldn't afford it. They bought premises in a run-down part of Old Trafford. Customers will travel anywhere for good food, he reasoned. Jean-Luc had no problems with moving to Manchester.

*   *   *

Bob walked round to the brick terraced house in Colley Street, selected the key and let himself in. His parents switched off the television and stood up from the settee to greet him. They hugged him as they hadn't seen him for years.

"To what do we owe this great honour?" said Brogan, in an accent that hadn't changed since he left Ballymote, in Sligo, fifty years before.

"It's only been a couple of weeks," Da.

"Couple 'o months, more like."

"Cup 'o tea?" asks Aoife.

"Yes, Mammy."

"Cake?"

"I never refuse your cake."

Brogan and Bob sat down. Bob took a hundred pounds from his wallet and handed it to his father. "What's this?' asked Brogan. I hope you've not been gambling."

"It's what I owe you."

"You don't owe me anything."

"I borrowed it to go to France."

"That was more than 20 years ago. I don't want it back."

"I want you to have it, Da. It's important to me."

"That's very touching, son. You've developed into a fine man with high moral principles. If accepting it means so much to you, then I accept it."

"I really appreciate it, Da. You see, you said that you'd never lend me anything ever again until I repaid it … so, can you lend me a grand, or maybe a bit more. I need a holiday."

Bob booked a late deal and flew off into the sun two days later. The same morning, Jean-Luc arrived at the restaurant in a small van and put a notice in the window: "Closed for refurbishment. Re-opens March 30th." He unloaded the vehicle and carried in dust sheets, cold chisel, hammer, bags of plaster, lime putty, buckets, skimming trowel, a rolled up piece of tracing paper bearing an image that was to become his next masterpiece, a bag of charcoal dust, pigments, lime, mortar & pestle, artists pallets and brushes and a toothed tracing wheel – like one of the wheels in the restaurant kitchen used for cutting pastry. He rolled up the carpet, put the tables and chairs to one side of the restaurant and covered everything with dust sheets. He put a ladder up to the wall that divided the restaurant from the kitchen. With a chisel and hammer he smashed off about two square metres of plaster, exposing the brick.

Then he began to replaster, working most of the time on a ladder. First, went on a layer of conventional plaster, then a layer of lime putty, skimmed smooth. He covered the newly plastered area with the tracing paper, taping it to the old plaster round the perimeter. He worked for five days without leaving the restaurant, sleeping on the floor from 2 a.m. to 5.30 a.m. each day. He stopped work only to make coffee and to make the odd snack. After five days four hours and three minutes, the masterpiece was finished – a copy of Crucifixion of the Capuchin by Guido Reni. The following day he re-decorated the wall around it. A day later, he cleaned the restaurant, relaid the carpet and put things back to normal, except that Christ on the cross, looked down upon the tables.

For the next two days, he wrote letters to bishops and to the press in the name of Audrey Williams, Nigel Holden, Donna Reid, Antonio Mundel, Pat Quinn, Siobháin Flaherty, Lee and Susie Hewitt, Donna Edge, John Shannon, Terry Stevens, Kevin Ridings and many more. He used his left hand to write some letters, some written with a fountain pen, some with ball point, others with felt tip, in different styles of hand-writing. He wrote others on his computer, printed out in different fonts, on an assortment of papers. He posted them in different districts, over three days in an assortment of envelopes. He set up numerous false e-mail addresses and wrote to the Church and the press in fictitious names about his masterpiece.

*   *   *

The Roman Catholic Bishop of Salford, Brendan McBishop, was tucking into a fried breakfast at his home in Wardley Hall. His chaplain, Fergal, was eating cereal. 'So how was the retreat, bishop?"

"The 'F' word springs to mind, Fergal'

"Freezing or frugal?

"Both, even at this time of year, but a nice bunch at Ampleforth."

"I guessed that when you asked for a fried breakfast. Things had been a bit Spartan."

"Much happened while I've been away?"

"The Evening News and the Metro have been trying to get you for an opinion."

"Didn't you put them through to Connor?"

"They don't want a communications officer. They want you. It's a theological matter. Blasphemy. Related to which, we've had a bag full of letters from complaining about the matter. Apparently, there's a restaurant in old Trafford with a fresco of the crucifixion."

*   *   *

Jean-Luc walked up to the counter at Aleef's news agents where there was a pile of copies of the Manchester Evening News. He picked up one and handed Shabir the money. He knew what to expect. The previous day, he had allowed reporters and photographers into the restaurant. There it was – the headline: *Blasphemy in Old Trafford.*

It continued: *Manchester's churches condemn a fresco in a Manchester restaurant and urge the Crown Prosecution Service to invoke the ancient blasphemy law.*

Bob arrived back from holiday, oblivious to what Jean-Luc had been up to. It was the day before the restaurant was due to reopen. Jean-Luc phoned him to say that they were fully booked for the reopening. The following morning at around ten O'clock, Bob drew up in the company's small van with fresh produce for the kitchen, but outside were a few dozen people, many wearing Manchester United scarves and shirts. As he approached the door, they surrounded him, "Can we "ave a look, mate?"
　　A look? What had Jean-Luc been up to?
　　"Not until *I've* had a look!" He unlocked the door, but he couldn't keep them out. They pushed him through the doorway, crashed inside and were agape … as was Bob.

"Awesome! Awesome" they said. One man crossed himself. Another knelt down and gazed at the Guido Reni's crucifixion. "Awesome".

"I knew that bugger was up to something," breathed Bob. When the crowd had gone, he found a copy of a newspaper on the bar. The headline read: "*Cantona Blasphemy Outrage!*" And there on the front page was a picture of Jean-Luc's painting.

Church leaders have condemned the fresco as blasphemous. The restaurant owner, Jean-Luc Cantona, who claims to be the second cousin of the former footballer, has defended the fresco. "Go to Florence, Venice, even the Vatican," he said, "And the depictions of Christ are all faces of people known at the time."

The Roman Catholic Bishop of Salford said, 'The difference between those old masterpieces and the restaurant fresco is that football fans refer to Mr. Cantona as *Le Dieu*! They even had posters and T-Shirts with his image and the words, *Le Dieu*. That is the context for this blasphemy. Eric Cantona depicted as Christ is blasphemy."

Bob wasn't keen on the fresco, but he loved the idea of a fully booked restaurant. At five O'clock that afternoon, a different crowd arrived, final-year students from catering and hospitality courses – waiters, sommeliers and kitchen helpers. Jean-Luc gathered them at the restaurant tables. "Thank you all for coming. You will be paid cash at the end of the evening, minimum wage, but all tips will be shared among you. Now, a few things. Sommelier – any wine on the menu under £40 a bottle is unavailable. Waiters – we don't do *well-done*. If they ask for it, tell them politely that *Row-Bair!* is one of the best chefs in the country. If they don't like his food, there are dozens of people who would love a table tonight. And now you Sou-chefs - Robert will brief you in the kitchen.

"I'll be asking for a volunteer to answer the phone and take bookings for future dates. We are fully booked for the next two weeks. And you, Sir." He said pointing to a tall overweight young man. "I want you on the door. No one comes in if they haven't got a reservation. I don't want voyeurs spoiling the evening. If anyone wants to see the fresco, they can book a table for a future occasion."

The evening went well. There were no complaints about the price of wine, nor about undercooked steak. When customers and helpers had gone, Jean-Luc turned the open sign to closed and printed out the total for the night – eight thousand, and sixty three pounds and twenty two pence. He and Bob sat at the bar, lit cigarettes and opened their own bottle of Bollinger.

The restaurant was full for the next two weeks, but towards the end of May bookings were tailing off a little. They were almost full at weekends, but only half full during the week. "At this rate of decline, we'll be empty at Christmas," said Bob. Then on the evening of June 21st Siobháin Hannon and her boyfriend, Luke, were at the table under the fresco, enjoying roast breast of quail with truffle fettuccine, and a pata negra pasta dish. All was pleasant in the restaurant when Siobháin let out a scream so loud that it almost shattered the windows. Then there was silence – not the chink of a glass nor the sound of cutlery on a plate. Even the waiters stood still.

With terror in her eyes and her mouth wide open, Siobháin's arm was outstretched towards the fresco. The hands and feet of Christ were bleeding.

Pope Francis was kneeling in prayer in his private chapel in front of the altar. Next to him was Javier. Both men lifted their eyes above the altar to the painting of *El Dios* – Diego Maradonna. "Javier. We must do something about the Usurper." There is only one God.

*   *   *

The Bishop of Salford was at his desk. Fergal knocked on the door and walked straight in. "Blood Group O rhesus positive . The Vatican and the press want you to contact them."

Television, press and radio bombarded the restaurant. A cordon of gold coloured rope now kept customers more than a metre from the fresco. Under the fresco, burned an altar candle. Jean-Luc gave daily press briefings for journalists from all over the world. One of his young staff shielded him from phone calls and took bookings. There was soon no availability till the end of August.

On the morning of 22 June, Eric Cantona flew into Manchester. He knew of the fresco, but was not prepared for the army of reporters and photographers that awaited his arrival. As he pushed through them, he said nothing and kept his head down. The crowd chanted, "Le Dieu! Le Dieu! Le Dieu!"

Next morning, he turned up to open a shelter for homeless people. He was on the pavement outside the shelter, standing by the ribbon. Press and television crews were there and so were a few hundred members of the public and officials. He began, "I am not going to answer questions about the fresco. I am here for the homeless," but before he could say any more, a woman, holding a baby, pushed through the crowd.

"Please touch my baby. He is very sick."

Cantona looked aghast and recoiled. "Get zis woman away! I must be in the plot of a film or I'm going mad!" The woman then thrust the baby against him. Others came out of the crowd, hobbling or in wheelchairs."

"You're my last hope, please, please. I beg you, help me!"

Cantona took the ribbon in both hands, snapped it. "I declare ze 'omeless centre open."

Then he sprinted to an awaiting car, mobbed by press, television and those who could run. His next appointment involved firing the gun at the start of a sponsored swim in the Salford Quays' basin, but before he had got there, local radio broadcasted an interview with the woman who had the sick baby. "Le Dieu has cured my baby".

The sick, the lame and the dying poured in their hundreds to the Salford Quays basin. Eric was warned and stayed away, but his voice and the sound of the gun were broadcast over the public address system from a remote location.

That evening, Eric Cantona phoned Sir Alex Ferguson at his Cheshire home to say that he would be late for dinner. At 8 p.m. all was going well at the Marseillaise. Bookings had been pouring in again. Most of the customers had arrived and some had begun their first course. The pleasant atmosphere was then shattered as the door was smashed open. It had not been locked, but an enraged man, had run at it and booted it open. Eric Cantona stood in the doorway, holding a pick axe. He stormed to the table nearest the fresco where a couple were enjoying hors d'oevre. With the pick axe in one hand, Cantona took hold of the table cloth with the other and dragged all that was on it to the floor. He kicked over the cordon, dragged the table up to the fresco and leaped on it. He raised the pick axe over his head, and smashed it into the work of art. With one blow after another, the plasterwork and the face of Christ cascaded to the ground. Cantona paused and then threw the pick axe onto the carpet. He jumped down and sped to Ryan Giggs car outside, leaving the customers staring at the damage. Where the hands and feet of Christ had been, dangled four plastic tubes, dripping blood.

Within an hour, television cameras were there. On BBC News 24 Clive Myree gave breaking news, "The fresco at the Marseillaise restaurant, thought to be miraculous, is a hoax. In a dramatic act of vandalism, Eric Cantona smashed into the plaster, revealing plastic tubes through which the restaurant owner's own blood had been fed. The tubes led to a room above the restaurant where Jean-Luc Cantona, who is believed to be a distant relative of the former footballer, controlled the flow of blood. We now join our reporter with Jean-Luc Cantona live at the restaurant."

Reporter: "You went to considerable lengths to gain publicity for your restaurant. Has it been worth it?"

Jean-Luc: "Most certainly. We serve the best food in all of Manchester. Before the fresco, nobody knew of us. In addition to publicity about the fresco, we have had outstanding reviews by food critics. The fresco is unimportant. It's the food that counts."

Reporter: "Where did you get the blood?"

Jean-Luc: "It was mine, extracted at a private clinic. It told them I was couriering it to a relative injured while on holiday in India."

Reporter: "What are your plans for the ruined

fresco?"

Jean-Luc: "I will restore it without the tubes. It is an important part of our restaurant history."

Two days later, Bob presented his ticket at the turnstiles and entered the ground he loved. The two teams filed onto the pitch, holding the hands of young mascots. Eric Cantona and a radio DJ were the team captains and stood together as the referee spun the coin. Eric won the toss. Moments later, he kicked off, passing the ball to one of the school of 92 who dribbled the ball past a number of eminent former footballers and took a shot at goal and scored.

The game continued with Eric Cantona scoring five goals. It seemed like a set-up, but nobody minded. It was good entertainment and raised a lot of money for local charities. Many of the fans were wearing Cantona shirts, bearing the words, *le Dieu!* Others displayed banners with the same words.

With five minutes of the game remaining, Eric Cantona was tackled and fell to the ground. He rolled over onto his back, clutching both feet. Two medics and stretcher bearers ran onto the pitch. They unlaced his boots. Cameras zoomed in with the images shown on the large screens in the ground. Off came both socks and then eighty thousand people went silent. There was not even the rustle of clothing. Not the flap of a bird's wing, nor the sound of a footstep. One of the paramedics recoiled and crossed himself. Tens of thousands in the ground, Catholics and non-Catholics alike, genuflected and crossed themselves also. Music, loud and majestic, broke the silence and flooded the ground. It Handel's Messiah's, "Behold the lamb of God, behold the lamb of God, who takes away the sin of the world."

Eric Cantona's feet were bleeding. All could see the nail holes, displayed on the screens, the wounds of Christ, the stigmata. He was carried from the pitch on the stretcher, with one arm hanging low, like the crucified Christ, being taken to the tomb.

Pope Francis was next to Javier in his private chapel, looking at the painting of *El Dios*.

"Javier, *we* have been the heretics."

"Yes Jorge, but substitutes are allowed in the beautiful game."

"Bring off number ten and send on number seven."

Javier took the painting from above the altar and replaced it. His Holiness murmured, "Oo Ah…"

OWN GOAL

Cast

Jason: 10 years old & a wizard with a football.

George: 35, Jason's father, bricklayer, usually wears working clothes - overalls, boots.

Mrs. Crab: 75, widow, sour, hates children, lives opposite Jason & George, wears pinafore and turban.
Park Keeper: 50, uniformed.

Teenage Boy 1: 13 years old, inner city kid.

Teenage Boy 2: 14 years old, inner city kid.

Scenes/Sets

Street:

The street of terraced houses where Jason and George live opposite Mrs. Crab. There is no traffic unless indicated in the script. When Jason plays in the street, he does so in the roadway between his house and Mrs. Crab's.

Jason's Bedroom:

Small with single bed, poor quality chest of drawers, football poster on the wall.

Kitchen:

George & Jason's Kitchen, scruffy, cluttered, but with a television.

Park:

An open area of grass. A tree, with a tall, broad trunk. A 'No Ball Games' sign is in the foreground.

SCENE 1   SATURDAY MORNING
STREET

JASON (GEORGE & MRS CRABB OFF SET)

JASON IS IN THE MIDDLE OF THE ROAD
PRACTISING HIS BALL SKILLS. HE KICKS
THE BALL HIGH AND CATCHES IT ON THE
BACK OF HIS NECK. HE KICKS THE BALL
ALOFT AGAIN AS IF TO REPEAT THE SAME
STUNT. AS THE BALL SOARS, GEORGE
OPENS THE FRONT DOOR, EXCITEDLY.

GEORGE:

Jason, you've got a trial.

JASON PUNCHES THE AIR AND KICKS THE
DESCENDING BALL ON THE VOLLEY, AS IF
SCORING A GOAL, BREAKING MRS
CRABB'S WINDOW. JASON & GEORGE GAPE
IN HORROR. MRS CRABB OPENS THE
DOOR.

SCENE 2 LATE SATURDAY AFTERNOON,
SAME DAY AS THE LAST SCENE.
JASON'S BEDROOM

JASON & GEORGE

JASON IS LYING ON HIS BED FULLY
CLOTHED, CRYING. GEORGE IS STANDING

OVER HIM.

GEORGE:

Have you done your homework?

JASON:

I haven't got any.

GEORGE:

Why don't you watch telly?

JASON:

Boring. (PAUSE) I want to practise for the trial.

GEORGE:

PAUSE

Look! I'll give you your ball back, but play with it in the park. If I see you as much as bounce it in the street, I'll cut it in shreds and tan your arse. It's costing me fifty bloody quid to have that window repaired.

<u>SCENE 3 LATE SATURDAY AFTERNOON,
TEN MINUTES AFTER LAST SCENE.</u>
<u>STREET</u>

A GLAZIER IS PUTTING THE FINISHING
TOUCHES TO MRS CRABB'S WINDOW.
GEORGE AND JASON LEAVE THEIR HOUSE.
JASON IS CARRYING HIS BALL. HE WALKS
UP THE STREET. GEORGE STANDS BY THE
FRONT DOOR, HOLDING HIS WALLET.

GEORGE:

(SHOUTING TO JASON) Don't so much as
bounce it before you get to the park.

JASON:

Yes, dad.

GEORGE WALKS TOWARDS THE GLAZIER,
OPENS HIS WALLET AND BEGINS TO COUNT
OUT BANK NOTES.

SCENE 4 LATE SATURDAY AFTERNOON
SHORTLY AFTER THE LAST SCENE
PARK

JASON IS PRACTISING HIS BALL SKILLS IN
THE PARK, NOT FAR FROM A SIGN WHICH
READS 'NO BALL GAMES.' HIS SKILL IS
SPECTACULAR. HE USES THE TRUNK OF A
TREE AS GOAL. HE IS ACROBATIC,
HEADING AND KICKING GOALS ONTO THE
SMALL TARGET AREA OF THE TREE TRUNK.

WHILE HE PRACTISES, THE PARK KEEPER
APPROACHES FROM FAR OFF, WALKING IN
THE MANNER OF A COPPER ON THE BEAT.
HE APPROACHES JASON AND, WITHOUT A
WORD, IN SILENT MOVIE STYLE, POINTS TO
THE SIGN AND SENDS JASON HOME.

SCENE 5   LATE SATURDAY AFTERNOON
SOON AFTER THE LAST SCENE.
STREET

JASON   & TEENAGE BOYS 1 & 2

JASON IS AT THE TOP OF HIS STREET,
CARRYING HIS FOOTBALL, HEADING FOR
HOME. TEENAGE BOYS 1 & 2 ARE WALKING
TOWARDS HIM AND THEN STAND IN HIS
WAY.

TEENAGE BOY 1:

Give us a kick.

JASON:

Mi dad 'ud kill me.

TEENAGE BOY 2:

HE PUNCHES THE BALL DOWNWARDS OUT
OF JASON'S HANDS.

Your dad won't know.

TEENAGE BOY 2 SNATCHES THE BALL ON
THE FIRST BOUNCE AND BOOTS IT UP THE
STREET IN THE DIRECTION OF JASON'S
HOUSE. AT THE SAME TIME, A BLACK BMW
DRIVES INTO THE BOTTOM OF THE STREET
AT SPEED, DRIVEN BY A YOUNG MAN. LOUD
MUSIC IS EMANATING FROM THE VEHICLE.
THE VEHICLE HITS THE BOUNCING BALL
AND KNOCKS IT THROUGH MRS CRABB'S

WINDOW. THE CAR SPEEDS OFF AND THE
TEENAGE BOYS RUN AWAY.

SCENE 6 LATER
KITCHEN

GEORGE   JASON

GEARGE IS FURIOUS, HOLDING JASON'S
BALL. JASON IS CRYING. GEORGE TAKES A
KITCHEN KNIFE AND DESTROYS THE
FOOTBALL.

JASON:

(CRYING) Mi Mam wouldn't 'ave done that.

GEORGE:

Don't say that! She buggered off. I am your
mam, now.

SCENE 7   MONDAY LATE EVENING
KITCHEN

NEWSCASTER (ON TELEVISION)   GEORGE

MR ROBERTS (ON THE PHONE)

GEORGE IS WASHING UP WHILE WATCHING THE NEWS.

NEWSCASTER:

Isidrio Gonzales, the Argentine international, has signed for Manchester United. (THE PHONE BEGINS TO RING. GEORGE DRIES HIS HANDS, BUT IS ABSORBED BY THE TELEVISION) Gonzales cost 90 million pounds and will be paid two hundred and twenty thousand pounds a week. (GEORGE MUTES THE TELEVISION AND ANSWERS THE PHONE) Yeh!

MR ROBERTS:

It's Mr. Roberts, Jason's Teacher. Would you mind if Jason stayed behind after school for a couple hours of football practise Mondays and Thursdays?

GEORGE:

It's better than 'im playing in the street.

MR ROBERTS:

He's got great talent. He'll play for United one day. (BOTH MEN PUT THE PHONE DOWN)

GEORGE:

Two hundred and Twenty thousand pounds a week!

SCENE 8   17:30 HOURS ON A WEEK DAY

JASON   GEORGE (OFF SET)

JASON HAS A TWOPENNY PIECE BALANCED ON THE TOE OF HIS SHOE. HE FLICKS IT UP AND CATCHES IT ON HIS FOREHEAD. HE CONTINUES DOING STUNTS WITH THE COIN, AS IF HE WERE PLAYING WITH A FOOTBALL. GEORGE ROUNDS THE CORNER OF THE STREET AND APPROACHES ON HIS WAY HOME FROM WORK. HE HAS HIS HAND BEHIND HIS BACK. JASON SEES HIM AND RUNS TOWARDS HIM.

JASON:

Have you got something for me?

GEORGE NODS AND GRINS.

Is it a ball?

GEORGE:

If you're gonna be good enough to earn
£220,000 a week, you'll need some practice.

HE PROUDLY PULLS HIS HAND FROM
BEHIND HIS BACK AND OFFERS JASON A
BEACH BALL. JASON'S FACE FALLS.

JASON:

I can't practise for the trial with that!

GEORGE:

You'd bloody-well better. I've paid good money
for it!

GEORGE GOES INSIDE. JASON PRACTISES
BUT HIS HEART ISN'T IN IT. MRS CRABB
COMES TO THE DOOR LOOKING MENACING.

SCENE 9   LATER IN THE KITCHEN

GEORGE   JASON (OFF SET)

GEORGE IS PUTTING BAKED BEANS IN THE

MICROWAVE. ENTER JASON.

GEORGE:

I thought I told you to bloodywell practise.

JASON:

The old crab won't let me.

GEORGE:

MAKING FOR THE DOOR.

We'll see about that! I'll show the interfering old cow!

SCENE 10   MOMENTS LATER IN THE STREET

GEORGE AND JASON ARE HAVING FUN HEADING THE BALL TO EACH OTHER RIGHT OUTSIDE MRS CRABB'S FRONT DOOR. MRS CRABB OPENS THE DOOR, LIVID. JASON

AND GEORGE PAY NO IMMEDIATE
ATTENTION.

GEORGE:

(TO HIMSELF OUTLOUD) If you can't get a life,
don't stop others from getting one.

MRS CRABB:

You can say what you like, but you're not going
to play ball in this street. (GEORGE CATCHES
THE BALL AND TURNS TO MRS CRABB.)

GEORGE:

What a sad old woman you are Mrs. Crab. You
love to hate the human race. This ball couldn't
break a window if it was fired from a cannon.

MRS CRABB:

I've 'eard it all before. Look what happened last

time.

GEORGE:

I'll prove it to you. I'm going to kick this ball, hard
as I can, at your window. It can't break it.

(SHE STANDS BETWEEN HIM AND THE
WINDOW WITH ARMS FOLDED)

MRS CRABB:

Over my dead body.

GEORGE:

Now there's a pleasing thought!

MRS CRABB:

(SHE TRIES TO SNATCH THE BALL)

Give me that ball!

GEORGE PASSES THE BALL TO JASON WHO
DARTS IN CIRCLES WITH MRS CRABB
CHASING HIM. GEORGE AND JASON ARE IN
HYSTERICS PASSING THE BALL TO EACH
OTHER AS MRS CRABB TRIES TO
INTERCEPT IT. WHEN MRS CRABB IS
TWENTY YARDS FROM HER FRONT DOOR,
JASON PASSES THE BALL TO GEORGE WHO
RUNS TOWARDS MRS CRABB'S WINDOW.

GEORGE:

Here you are, you old bizzum. This ball couldn't
break a spider's web.

AS HE KICKS THE BALL AT HER WINDOW,
HIS BOOT FLIES OFF, AND SAILS THROUGH
THE AIR IN THE DIRECTION OF THE
WINDOW.